Good Night, Knight

ALSO BY BETSY LEWIN

Thumpy Feet

★ "Anyone who has ever known and loved a cat will be instantly captivated by Lewin's fun-loving feline creation."
—*Kirkus Reviews* (starred review)

You Can Do It!

A BANK STREET COLLEGE OUTSTANDING CHILDREN'S BOOK
"Each gesture and eye movement conveys the intense drama of a young creature struggling for confidence and accomplishment."—*School Library Journal*

Good Night, Knight

Betsy Lewin

I Like to Read®

Holiday House / New York

To Baby Ellis, Welcome to the world!

I LIKE TO READ is a registered trademark of Holiday House, Inc.

Copyright © 2015 by Betsy Lewin
All Rights Reserved
HOLIDAY HOUSE is registered in the U.S. Patent and Trademark Office.
Printed and Bound in October 2014 at Tien Wah Press, Johor Bahru, Johor, Malaysia.
The artwork was created with Sharpie pen and watercolor on Strathmore kid finish paper.
www.holidayhouse.com
First Edition
1 3 5 7 9 10 8 6 4 2

Library of Congress Cataloging-in-Publication Data
Lewin, Betsy, author, illustrator.
Good night, Knight / Betsy Lewin. — First edition.
pages cm — (I like to read)
Summary: After a tantalizing dream about golden cookies, Knight and his horse embark on a quest for baked goods.
ISBN 978-0-8234-3206-6 (hardcover)
[1. Knights and knighthood—Fiction. 2. Horses—Fiction. 3. Cookies—Fiction.] I. Title.
PZ7.L58417Go 2015
[E]—dc23
2014007376

ISBN 978-0-8234-3315-5 (paperback)

Knight said,
"Good night, Horse."

Horse said,
"Good night, Knight."

Horse went to sleep.

Knight went to sleep.

Knight had a dream.

Knight woke up.
He woke up Horse.

Knight climbed on Horse.
Clank! Clank!

Horse trotted.
Clip-clop!

Knight said, "Whoa!"
He looked in the hole.
No golden cookies.

He sat on Horse.
Clank! Clank!

Horse trotted.
Clip-clop!

Knight said,
"Whoa!"
He looked in the bushes.
No golden cookies.

He climbed on Horse.
Clank! Clank!

Horse trotted.
Clip-clop!

Knight said, "Whoa!"
He looked in the water.
No golden cookies.

Knight said,
"I am sleepy.
Let's go home."
He climbed
on Horse.
Clank! Clank!
Horse trotted.
Clip-clop!

Knight said,
"I am *very* sleepy."
Horse stopped.
Knight fell off.

Clank!
Clank!

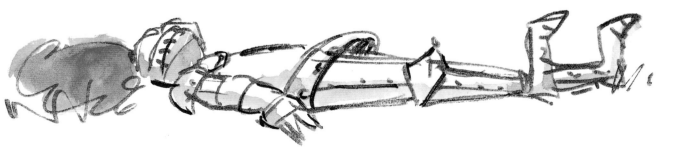

Horse said,
"Wake up, Knight!
We are home."

Knight said,
"Good night, Horse."

Horse said,
"Good night, Knight."

Horse went to sleep.
Knight went to sleep.

You will like these too!

Come Back, Ben *by Ann Hassett and John Hassett*
A KIRKUS REVIEWS BEST BOOK

Dinosaurs Don't, Dinosaurs Do *by Steve Björkman*
A NOTABLE SOCIAL STUDIES TRADE BOOK FOR YOUNG PEOPLE
AN IRA/CBC CHILDREN'S CHOICE

Fish Had a Wish *by Michael Garland*
A KIRKUS REVIEWS BEST BOOK
A TOP 25 CHILDREN'S BOOKS LIST BOOK

The Fly Flew In *by David Catrow*
AN IRA/CBC CHILDREN'S CHOICE
MARYLAND BLUE CRAB YOUNG READER AWARD WINNER

Look! *by Ted Lewin*
THE CORRELL BOOK AWARD FOR EXCELLENCE
IN EARLY CHILDHOOD INFORMATIONAL TEXT

Mice on Ice *by Rebecca Emberley and Ed Emberley*
A BANK STREET BEST CHILDREN'S BOOK OF THE YEAR
AN IRA/CBC CHILDREN'S CHOICE

Pig Has a Plan *by Ethan Long*
AN IRA/CBC CHILDREN'S CHOICE

See Me Dig *by Paul Meisel*
A KIRKUS REVIEWS BEST BOOK

See Me Run *by Paul Meisel*
A THEODOR SEUSS GEISEL AWARD HONOR BOOK
AN ALA NOTABLE CHILDREN'S BOOK

See more I Like to Read® books.
Go to www.holidayhouse.com/I-Like-to-Read/